PAUL BUNYAN
AND HIS BIG BLUE OX

Retold by
VIRGINIA SCHOMP

Illustrated by
JESS YEOMANS

Cavendish
Square

New York

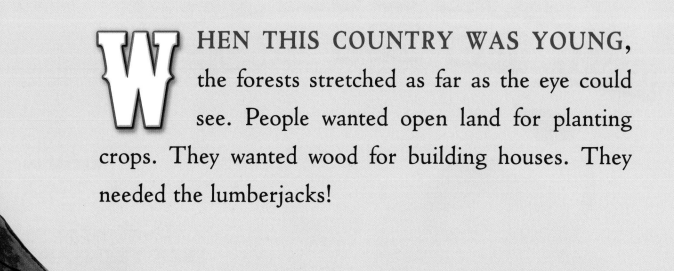

WHEN THIS COUNTRY WAS YOUNG, the forests stretched as far as the eye could see. People wanted open land for planting crops. They wanted wood for building houses. They needed the lumberjacks!

2

The lumberjacks worked hard in the deep woods. They chopped down trees and hauled logs till the stars came out. Then they sat around a crackling campfire. They told tales of old logging days, when everything was extra big, even the men. And of course, they remembered the biggest, strongest lumberjack of them all, Paul Bunyan.

Some folks say that Paul Bunyan was the biggest baby ever born. It took five giant storks to deliver him to his parents. The first time he cried, the birds fell out of the trees. After that, all the forest critters wore earmuffs.

When Paul was three weeks old, he sneezed. *Splat!* The blast flattened the neighbors' houses. So his parents built a new log cradle. They floated the cradle out in the ocean, where their supersized son could stay out of trouble.

Paul loved his new bed. He giggled. He wriggled. He rocked back and forth in the water. *Whoosh!* He set off a tidal wave that flooded villages all along the coast.

Paul kept growing…and growing…and growing. It sure was hard to keep that growing boy fed. Every morning, his ma cooked up a dozen eggs and ten pots of oatmeal. After that little snack, Paul was ready for breakfast.

His parents also worked hard to keep him in clothes. Once a month, his pa carved a new pair of shoes from two pine trees. His ma used the wool from a whole flock of sheep to knit her son a sweater. How did she make the buttons? She sewed on the wheels from a wagon!

School was not easy for a husky young fellow like Paul. By third grade, he was too big for the schoolhouse. Instead of going into class, he had to sit outside and peek through the window.

Paul liked learning to read and write. But when he practiced his ABCs, he wore out all the pencils. So his teacher made a special rule. She wrote it on the blackboard:

Attention! No student shall write any word with more than three letters, except as a treat on their birthday. This rule applies to all boys and girls over 50 feet tall named Paul Bunyan.

One snowy day, Paul was walking home from school. It was so cold that his teeth were chattering and his lips were blue. Why, even the snow was turning blue! Soon the world wore a sparkly blanket of sky blue snow.

Paul saw a strange, lumpy hill. It had two furry ears. He grabbed the ears and pulled. Out popped a little lost ox, as cold and blue as the snow.

The boy wrapped his warm scarf around the shivering ox. "Poor little babe," he said. Later, Babe gave Paul a playful kick that knocked him on his rear, just to say "Thanks!"

That little blue ox sure grew up fast. One night, Paul put him in the barn. The next morning, the ox *and* the barn were missing. Paul found Babe in a neighbor's yard, with the barn perched on his back.

By springtime, Babe was fully grown. He measured 42 ax handles from eye to eye. Some folks tried to reckon how long he was, but no one could count that high.

Paul knew that he and Babe must be meant for something BIG. So he said good-bye to his parents. Then Paul Bunyan and his big blue ox set out to see the world.

Paul and Babe headed west. By lunchtime, they had crossed over seven states. Whenever the big ox got thirsty, Paul would stop and dig out a water hole. Today we call those holes the Great Lakes.

After a few thousand miles, Paul began to get tired. He dragged his heavy ax behind him as he walked. When he stopped to rest, he saw that the ax had carved out a fine little ditch. "What a Grand Canyon!" he exclaimed. And the name has stuck ever since.

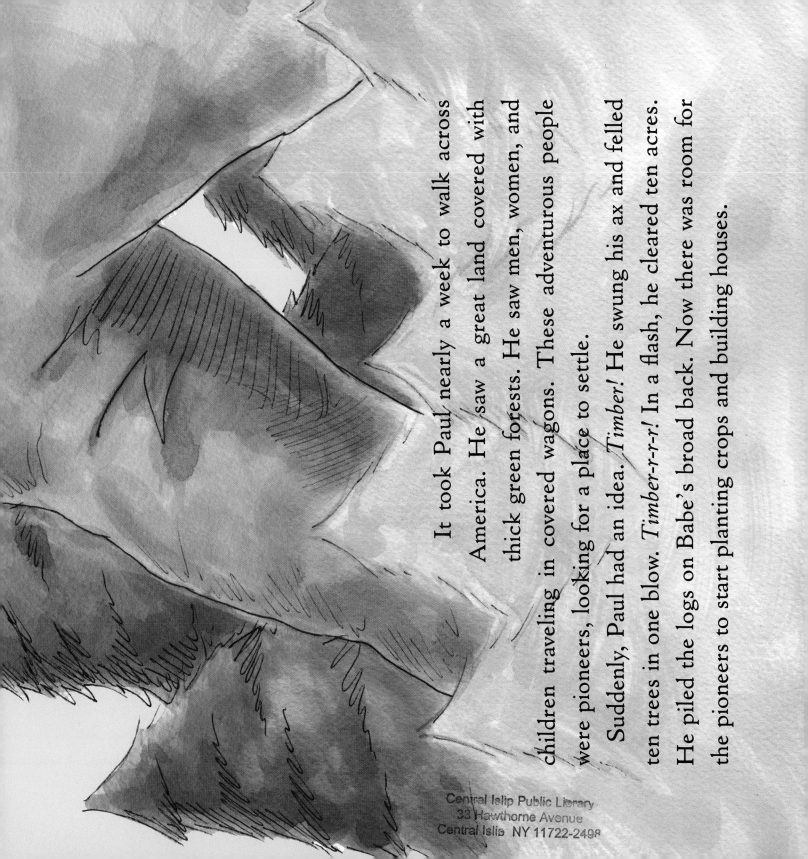

It took Paul nearly a week to walk across America. He saw a great land covered with thick green forests. He saw men, women, and children traveling in covered wagons. These adventurous people were pioneers, looking for a place to settle.

Suddenly, Paul had an idea. *Timber!* He swung his ax and felled ten trees in one blow. *Timber-r-r-r!* In a flash, he cleared ten acres. He piled the logs on Babe's broad back. Now there was room for the pioneers to start planting crops and building houses.

After Paul invented logging, he was famous.
Thousands of men wanted to work for him. So
he set up a giant camp for his lumberjacks. He
built the bunkhouse like a hotel. It was so tall that its
roof scraped the sky.

Some folks said that building was *too* tall. By the time
the men in the top bunks climbed up to bed, the breakfast
bell was ringing. "No problem!" Paul said. "The men
can float up on balloons at night and parachute down in
the morning!"

The head cook at the logging camp was Sourdough Sam. Each morning, Sam made pancakes on a huge iron frying pan. How did his helpers grease the giant pan? They tied bacon to their boots and skated back and forth.

The dining hall was ten miles long. Some of the lumberjacks nearly starved to death waiting for breakfast! So Paul invented roller skates. Now the waiters could zoom right down the middle of the table. Pancakes flew onto plates as fast as the hungry men could eat them. A pair of racehorses pulled the maple syrup wagon.

After breakfast, the lumberjacks were ready for work. Back then, the trees were so tough it could take a week just to chop through the bark. To help his men work faster, Paul invented a new kind of ax. It had two blades, so they could chop two trees at once.

Babe hauled the cut trees out of the woods. At first, the logging road caused all sorts of trouble. It twisted and turned just for fun, till the men riding out met themselves coming back in. Paul fixed that problem, too. He hitched Babe to the end of the crooked road, and the big ox pulled it straight.

Even the weather could be tricky in Paul Bunyan's time. One year, it was summer all winter long. Another time, all four seasons came at once. The whole camp had a bad case of spring fever-sunburn-flu-frostbite.

Worst of all was the year when two winters got stuck together. It was so cold that the campfires froze. The men tried to complain, but their words turned to ice. At least that made it easy for Paul to write home. He just packed up his frozen greetings and sent them through the mail. His parents put the package by the fire to thaw out. They sure were surprised to hear it say, "Howdy, folks! Moo!"

Paul's crew worked at logging for a long, long time. They roamed from coast to coast, clearing the land for settlers. Whenever it was time to move on, Babe hauled the camp down the road, just like an engine pulling a toy train set.

One day, Paul stopped and looked around. "My work is finished," he said. "I have done all I can to help build America." Then he and Babe wandered off in search of new adventures. Some folks say they are still wandering. Next time you are in the woods, listen closely. Do you hear a low rumble? That just might be Paul Bunyan calling to his faithful blue ox.

ABOUT PAUL BUNYAN

PAUL BUNYAN is about 150 years old. He was born in logging camps in Maine, Michigan, and other parts of North America. The loggers told stories to pass the long, chilly nights. Some of their tales were about real men. Others were about make-believe heroes. The stories (and the heroes) grew with each telling. In time, all these "tall tales" came together in the legend of Paul Bunyan.

Many of the vast forests that once covered America are gone. Today we wish that the old-time loggers had taken better care of the environment. But we can still enjoy the stories about America's favorite lumberjack. Paul Bunyan's adventures make us laugh. They also remind us of the hard work and spirit that made our country grow.

Our story of Paul Bunyan is based mainly on tall tales collected by Esther Shephard (1924), James Stevens (1925), and Harold W. Felton (1947).

WORDS TO KNOW

legend A story that has been passed down from earlier times. Legends may be based on real people and events, but they are not entirely true.

lumberjacks People who cut down trees and take the logs to a sawmill. Lumberjacks are also called loggers.

pioneers People who explored and settled the American West.

tall tale A funny, exaggerated story. Tall tales are unbelievable, but they are told as if they were true.

TO FIND OUT MORE

BOOKS

Harrison, David L. *Paul Bunyan: My Story*. New York: Random House, 2008.

Krensky, Stephen. *Paul Bunyan*. Minneapolis, MN: Millbrook Press, 2007.

Lorbiecki, Marybeth. *Paul Bunyan's Sweetheart*. Chelsea, MI: Sleeping Bear Press, 2007.

WEBSITES

American Folklore: Paul Bunyan

www.americanfolklore.net/paulbunyan.html

Storyteller S. E. Schlosser retells seven tall tales from Wisconsin, including "Birth of Paul Bunyan" and "Babe the Blue Ox."

Paul Bunyan in Flapjack Frenzy

www.animatedtalltales.com/flash/story

Here you can watch an animated retelling of a story about Paul's hungry crew. This site also has some fun interactive games.

Paul Bunyan: The Giant Lumberjack

www.paulbunyantrail.com/talltale.html

This illustrated story about the giant lumberjack's life is presented by the folks at the Paul Bunyan Trail in Minnesota.

ABOUT THE AUTHOR

VIRGINIA SCHOMP has written more than eighty books for young readers on topics including dinosaurs, dolphins, American history, and ancient myths. She lives among the tall pines of New York's Catskill Mountain region. She enjoys hiking, gardening, watching old movies on TV and new anime online, and, of course, reading, reading, and reading.

ABOUT THE ILLUSTRATOR

JESS YEOMANS was born and raised on Long Island, New York, and grew up with a love of art and animals. She received her Illustration BFA at the Fashion Institute of Technology. She has been featured in many exhibits and has been awarded numerous awards and honors for her artwork.

Jess works as a freelance illustrator in Brooklyn. She enjoys drawing and painting, snowboarding, animals, cooking, and being outdoors. To see more of her work, visit www.jessyeomans.com.

Published in 2014 by Cavendish Square Publishing, LLC
303 Park Avenue South, Suite 1247, New York, NY 10010

First Edition

Website: cavendishsq.com

This publication represents the opinions and views of the author based on his or her personal experience, knowledge, and research. The information in this book serves as a general guide only. The author and publisher have used their best efforts in preparing this book and disclaim liability rising directly or indirectly from the use and application of this book.

CPSIA Compliance Information: Batch #WS13CSQ

All websites were available and accurate when this book was sent to press.

LIBRARY OF CONGRESS CATALOGING-IN-PUBLICATION DATA
Schomp, Virginia.
Paul Bunyan and his big blue ox / retold by Virginia Schomp.
p. cm. — (American legends and folktales)
Summary: Relates some of the exploits of Paul Bunyan, a lumberjack said to
be taller than the trees whose pet was a blue ox named Babe.
Includes bibliographical references.
ISBN 978-1-60870-443-9 (hardcover) ISBN 978-1-62712-018-0 (paperback) ISBN 978-1-60870-609-9 (ebook)
1. Bunyan, Paul, (Legendary character)—Legends. [1. Bunyan, Paul,
(Legendary character)—Legends. 2. Folklore—United States. 3. Tall tales.] I. Title.
PZ8.1.S3535Pau 2010
398.20973´02—dc22
[E]
2010023520

EDITOR: Joyce Stanton
ART DIRECTOR: Anahid Hamparian   SERIES DESIGNER: Kristen Branch

Printed in the United States of America